JER Ritche
Ritchey, Kate
A perfect picnic /

34028083678772
STR $3.99 ocn834903231
10/14/13

D1043576

Your child is beginning the lifelong adventure of reading! And
with the **World of Reading** program, you can be sure that he or
she is receiving the encouragement needed to become a confident,
independent reader. This program is specially designed to
encourage your child to enjoy reading at every level by combining
exciting, easy-to-read stories featuring favorite characters with
colorful art that brings the magic to life.

The **World of Reading** program is divided into four levels so
that children at any stage can enjoy a successful reading experience:

Reader-in-Training
Pre-K–Kindergarten
Picture reading and word repetition for children who are getting
ready to read.

Beginner Reader
Pre-K–Grade 1
Simple stories and easy-to-sound-out words for children who are just
learning to read.

Junior Reader
Kindergarten–Grade 2
Slightly longer stories and more varied sentences perfect for children
who are reading with the help of a parent.

Super Reader
Grade 1–Grade 3
Encourages independent reading with rich story lines and wide
vocabulary that's right for children who are reading on their own.

Learning to read is a once-in-a-lifetime adventure, and with
World of Reading, the journey is just beginning!

Copyright © 2013 Disney Enterprises, Inc.
All rights reserved. Published by Disney Press, an imprint of Disney Book Group. No part of this book may
be reproduced or transmitted in any form or by any means, electronic or mechanical, including photocopying,
recording, or by any information storage and retrieval system, without written permission from the publisher.
For information address Disney Press, 114 Fifth Avenue, New York, New York 10011-5690.
Printed in the United States of America
First Edition
3 5 7 9 10 8 6 4 2
G658-7729-4-13088
Library of Congress Catalog Card Number: 2012936863
ISBN 978-1-4231-6963-5

For more Disney Press fun, visit www.disneybooks.com

If you purchased this book without a cover, you should be aware that this book is stolen property.
It was reported as "unsold and destroyed" to the publisher, and neither the author nor the publisher
has received any payment for this "stripped" book.

SUSTAINABLE
FORESTRY
INITIATIVE

Certified Chain of Custody
Promoting Sustainable Forestry
www.sfiprogram.org
SFI-01415
The SFI label applies to the text stock

Disney
MICKEY & FRIENDS

A Perfect Picnic

By Kate Ritchey
Illustrated by Loter, Inc. and the
Disney Storybook Artists

Disney PRESS
New York

It was a beautiful spring day.
The sun was shining and
the birds were singing.
Mickey and Pluto were planning
a picnic in the park.

"I have an idea," Mickey said.
"We should invite our friends
to the picnic!
We can all enjoy the sunshine
and share our favorite foods!"

Mickey called Goofy.
"Pluto and I are having a picnic,"
he told his friend.
"Would you like to come?"
Goofy agreed. A picnic was a
great way to spend the day!

"Bring your favorite fruit,
your favorite sandwich,
and your favorite drink,"
Mickey said.
"Then everyone can trade baskets."

Next, Mickey visited Minnie.
"We are having a picnic,"
he told her.
Minnie was excited.
She could not wait
to share her favorite foods!

Soon, Mickey found Donald and Daisy.
"A picnic sounds like a great idea,"
Daisy said.
"I know just what to make!"
Donald added.

At home, Donald started his lunch.
He took out two pieces of bread
to make a sandwich.
He got out his favorite drink.
Then he chose a piece of fruit.

But as he looked at the food,
Donald began to get hungry.
I do not <u>want</u> to share my lunch,
he thought.
I want to eat it myself!

Minnie was making lunch, too.
She put her drink into a jug.
She packed a piece of fruit.
Then she made her
favorite sandwich,
peanut butter!

As she got ready,
Minnie started to wonder
if she would like the other lunches.
I do not <u>want</u> to share my lunch,
she thought.
I want to eat it myself!

Daisy was excited about sharing
her lunch with her friends!
She hummed to herself as she
packed her sandwich and drink.
Then she picked up a banana.

Daisy thought of someone else
eating her favorite fruit.
I do not <u>want</u> to share my lunch,
she thought.
I want to eat it myself!

Over at Goofy's house,
the kitchen was very messy!
Goofy was making lemonade
to take to the picnic.
He was soaking wet and
covered in lemon juice!

Goofy tasted his lemonade.
It was delicious!
This is my best lemonade ever,
he thought.
I do not <u>want</u> to share it.
I want to drink it all by myself!

Mickey did not know that his friends
had changed their minds.
He was busy packing his basket.
"Is that everything, Pluto?"
he asked.

Pluto barked and whined.
"Thanks for reminding me,"
Mickey said.
"I would not want
to forget your lunch!"

Mickey finished filling his basket
and went to the park.
As he walked,
he sang to himself.

Mickey's friends were
waiting for him.
They all had baskets of food.
But they did not look happy.

"What is wrong?" Mickey asked.
"I do not want to share my lunch,"
Donald said.
"What if I do not like
the lunch I get?" Minnie asked.

Daisy and Goofy agreed.
Everyone wanted to eat
their own favorite foods.
"I guess we do not <u>have</u> to trade,"
Mickey said.

Minnie looked at Mickey.
He looked very sad.
She handed him her basket.
"I will trade with you, Mickey,"
she said.

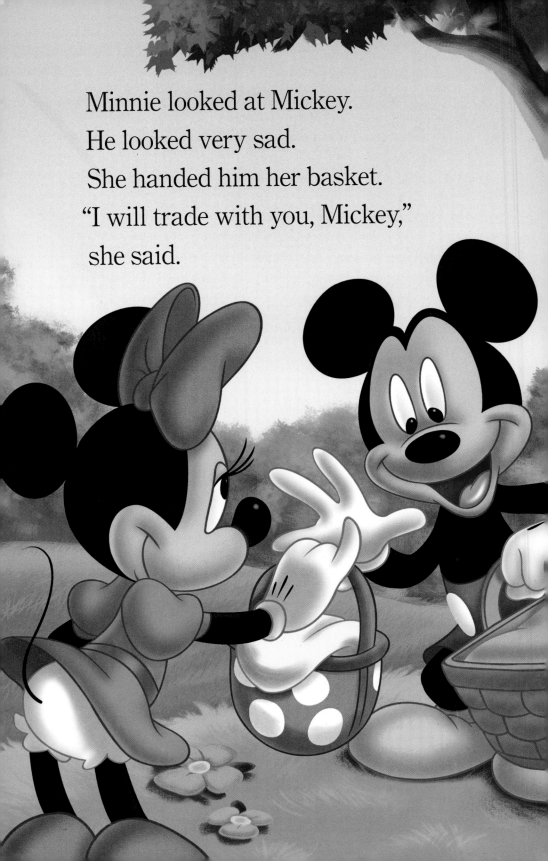

Mickey's friends saw that
Minnie had made Mickey happy.
They wanted to make Mickey happy, too.
"Will someone trade with me?"
Donald asked, holding out his lunch.
Soon, they had all swapped baskets.

Mickey laid out a blanket.
Minnie passed out plates.
Goofy handed out napkins.
Daisy gave everyone a cup.
Donald set out forks.
Finally, it was time to eat!

Mickey opened his basket first.
He started to laugh.
Donald looked in his basket
and laughed, too.
Everyone had packed lemonade
and peanut butter sandwiches!

But each basket had a different fruit.
Donald had a pineapple.
Daisy had grapes.
Minnie had an orange.
Goofy had a banana.
Mickey had an apple.

"How can we share our fruit?"
Minnie asked.
"I have an idea," Mickey said.
"Leave it to me!"

While everyone ate their sandwiches
and drank their lemonade,
Mickey cut up the fruit.
He put it all in a bowl
and mixed it together.

It was a big fruit salad!
Now everyone could try
their friends' favorite fruits.
"What a great way to share
what we like best," Daisy said.

Harris County Public Library
Houston, Texas

Mickey's friends agreed
as they ate their dessert.
It was the perfect end
to a perfect picnic!